W9-CKH-585

This Storybook Belongs to:

Princess _____

THE LITTLE MERMAID

Enchanted Moments

Advance
PUBLISHERS

Once upon a time, there was a Little Mermaid named Ariel who lived in a kingdom under the sea. Ariel was not happy being a mermaid. She longed to be part of the world far above the ocean floor—the human world.

Ariel even had her own collection of human things. She kept the objects in her secret grotto and would go there to admire them, imagining that she was human, too.

Ariel's father, King Triton, discovered that Ariel had been swimming to the ocean's surface. He was very upset with her, because contact with the human world was strictly forbidden.

The king put his court composer, Sebastian, in charge of his headstrong daughter. "Ariel needs someone to keep her out of trouble," the sea king explained. "And you are just the crab to do it!"

But Sebastian could not stop the determined Little Mermaid. One day, while swimming with her friend, Flounder, Ariel saw a ship floating on the surface of the water. She swam up to the ship and spied a handsome prince named Eric.

Sir Grimsby presented Eric with a statue of himself for a birthday present. Then he asked when the prince was going to think about marriage.

"Oh, come on, Grim," said Eric. "I just haven't found the right girl, yet. But she's out there somewhere. And when I find her, I'll know."

Suddenly, a terrible storm came up and Prince Eric fell overboard. Ariel dove underneath the crashing waves and pulled him to safety.

On the shore, she sang to Eric until Sir Grimsby came to rescue him.

"I heard a girl singing," Eric said. "She had a beautiful voice."

"I think you swallowed a bit too much seawater," said Grimsby, helping Eric to his feet.

When King Triton found out that Ariel had rescued Eric, he was furious. "Have you lost your senses?" King Triton asked. "He's a human; you're a mermaid. You could never be together!"

"But Daddy," Ariel protested, "I love him!"

King Triton was so furious that he destroyed Ariel's grotto and everything in it. "If this is the only way to get through to you, then so be it!"

Ariel looked around at what had once been her wonderful grotto and began to cry.

Suddenly she heard voices. "Poor child," hissed one.

"Poor sweet child," hissed another.

Ariel found herself surrounded by two slimy eels, Flotsam and Jetsam.

"We represent someone who can help you," said the eels. "Ursula can make all your dreams come true...."

Ariel choked back her tears. "The sea witch!" she cried.

Ariel, Flounder, and Sebastian went to see Ursula, the sea witch.

Ursula promised to turn Ariel into a human for three days in exchange for her voice. She explained that in order for Ariel to remain human, the prince would have to kiss her before the sun set on the third day. "Or, you turn back into a mermaid and you belong to me!" said Ursula, cackling.

Ariel nervously agreed. Sebastian and Flounder watched in horror as Ariel signed a contract with the sea witch.

The exchange was made, and Ursula captured Ariel's voice in a shell. Then wiggling and writhing, Ariel's tail transformed to become human legs.
On land, Ariel could not believe that her legs were real.

"Something's different about you," said her friend Scuttle the seagull.

"She's got legs!" cried Sebastian.

"She's got to make the prince fall in love with her," added Flounder.

All three friends agreed to help the Little Mermaid.

When Prince Eric and his dog, Max, found Ariel, he didn't recognize her. He only remembered the beautiful voice of the person who had rescued him.

"You can't speak?" he asked Ariel. "Oh, then you can't be who I thought you were…but don't worry, I'll help you."

The prince took Ariel home to his castle. On the second day of her visit, they toured his kingdom.

Sitting in the lagoon together, the moment came when Eric leaned over to kiss Ariel. But before he could kiss her, Flotsam and Jetsam made the boat overturn, and they fell into the water.

The sea witch had been watching in her crystal ball. "That was a close one!" said Ursula. "Too close. It's time for Ursula to take matters into her own tentacles!"

Using her black magic, Ursula changed herself into a beautiful maiden. She wore the shell that held Ariel's voice around her neck.

As soon as Eric heard the voice, he was hypnotized. He agreed to marry the maiden that very day aboard the royal wedding ship.

Ariel was beside herself when she heard the news. Luckily, Scuttle flew over-head and discovered the maiden's secret—she was the sea witch in disguise!

Scuttle and Flounder went into action while Sebastian went to get the sea king. Scuttle brought his friends aboard the ship and tried to stop the wedding. During their struggle, the maiden's necklace shattered. Eric awoke from his trance, and Ariel got her voice back.

"You're too late!" cried the sea witch as she watched Ariel turn back into a mermaid. Ursula grabbed her and jumped into the water.

"It's not you I'm after," she said to Ariel. "I've got a much bigger fish to fry."

Ursula saw King Triton swimming towards her. The king offered to change places with his daughter, and Ursula accepted.

"At last, these are mine!" she cried, grabbing his crown and magic trident. "Now I am ruler of all the ocean!"

Ursula did not know that Eric had followed Ariel into the sea. Steering an old sunken ship, Eric aimed the bow right into the wicked sea witch. Slowly, Ursula's enormous body sank beneath the waves.

Everything returned to the way it was. The ocean became calm once more, and King Triton's powers were restored.

The king looked over at his unhappy daughter. "She really does love him, doesn't she?" he asked Sebastian.

And, with a wave of his trident, King Triton changed Ariel's tail back into legs.

Sebastian, Flounder, King Triton, and all the merfolk watched as Ariel married Prince Eric.

At last, the Little Mermaid was part of the human world she loved so dearly, and she and her prince would live happily ever after.